Quick as a Dodo

Quick as a Dodo

BY

Ralph McInerny

WITH

ILLUSTRATIONS

BY

Pam Butterworth

THE VANGUARD PRESS

NEW YORK

Library of Congress Catalogue Card Number: 77–93301
ISBN: 0–8149–0794–6
Designer: Tom Bevans
Manufactured in the United States of America.

for Liz Christman

CONTENTS

Quick as
a Dodo

1

Who and What I Am

The picture window is a hazard to navigation. I speak, as I shall endeavor always to speak in this narrative, from direct experience. And I shall speak of many and wonderful things.

I am often asked what it feels like to be the only, doubtless the last, dodo on earth. The questioner is apt to eye me as if I were trying to market square circles or prove that yesterday will be tomorrow, but some, like yourself, ask out of a genuine desire to be instructed. Here, then, is my story, which will be fascinating to children from 7 to 11 and to adults from 11 to midnight.

To begin at the beginning, I was discovered by children who were on an Easter-egg hunt. One of them, a monster of a child named Sidney Morton, took me home and slipped me beneath his pillow. I would like to say that he did this out of compassion or because he was taken by the beauty of my shell. The truth is, he was simply hiding something he had stolen from the basket of another child. Having hidden me, he forgot me. I have often pondered the fact that I owe my life, at least in part, to larceny and forgetfulness.

In any case, warmed by Sidney's hot and fretful head and by the feather-filled pillow that might have been my sainted mother's bosom, I began to stir into life inside the shell that had encased me for perhaps a century or more. When I hatched, Sidney was delighted to have me, at least

at first. An old fur-lined slipper of Sidney's father became my bed. I had a pan of water in which to float about. I came to enjoy checkers, reading, and late snacks. I should add that Sidney had not told his parents that I was in the house. You will wonder how I could have been kept a secret. Would not Sidney's mother, coming into his room to make the bed, notice my rather noticeable self snoozing in a slipper in the closet? No. Sidney had an abominable temper and a species of truce obtained between him and his parents. His room was out of bounds to them, though I suspect that his mother preferred to think that Sidney was being punished, since the care of his room was left to him.

One night, quite late, I was rummaging about in the refrigerator when a piercing scream behind me caused me to jump in fright. The door of the refrigerator closed; the room was plunged into darkness. There was the sound of footsteps thundering up the stairs. The screaming continued. I recognized the voice as that of Sidney's mother.

"George," she screamed. "George!"

George apparently fell onto the floor as he clambered from bed. His shout of pain was added to his wife's screaming. Meanwhile, I remained motionless. Whatever had frightened Sidney's mother might be there in the kitchen with me.

"There is a—*thing* in the kitchen," Sidney's mother was blubbering. She and George had come to the top of the stairs and their voices were audible even though neither was shouting now.

"A thing? What kind of thing?"

"A horrible, horrible—oh, ugh!"

You can imagine my own fright now. Somewhere in the house, perhaps still in the kitchen with me, was this thing that had so frightened Sidney's mother.

"Was it a man, Flo?" George's voice trembled slightly. The stairway light went on, finally.

"No, it wasn't a man." Her normal contemptuous tone indicated that she found George's question ridiculous. I was relieved.

I heard them coming down the stairs then, George and Flo, and I stepped out of the kitchen. To my surprise, Flo began to scream again, and George himself stepped back, a strange expression on his face. Of course, I recognized the two of them from the photographs pinned to Sidney's dart board as well as from glimpses I had had of them from Sidney's window. Their reaction caused me to wheel about and look behind me. Nothing.

"Good Lord," George cried, "it's a bird."

"What kind of bird?"

"I don't know."

"He's mine." Sidney, awakened no doubt by all the noise, had appeared behind his parents on the stairs. "His name is Dormer and he belongs to me."

"Where did you get him?"

"How long have you had him?"

"You are not keeping that bird in my house," Sidney's mother said.

"I keep him in my room."

"I found him raiding the refrigerator."

"He gets hungry during the night."

(5)

Meanwhile, George Morton was edging down the stairs toward me, his eyes squinted, an odd smile on his lips.

"He's some kind of duck," he said.

"I am not a duck," I told him.

He stopped. "Do you speak English?"

I nodded. No reason not to oblige. I said, "English."

"Flo, listen to this. It talks. Say it again," George urged me. He came all the way downstairs and stooped to pat my head. I ducked.

"Duck is an intransitive verb meaning to lower the head swiftly, as when avoiding a thrown object or a low ceiling. I am not a duck."

George seemed fascinated by this information, though it was readily available to him in any standard dictionary.

"Leave him alone," Sidney said, joining his father. "Can't you see he's scared?"

"Get that thing out of my house," Flo Morton said. "I won't have that horrible thing in my house."

"You've got a parakeet," Sidney said.

George was studying me closely. "You're not a mallard," he told me. "You're not a canvasback."

Sidney said, "He's not a parakeet either. Come on, Dormer."

"I'm hungry," I said.

"What does he eat?" George asked.

"Everything."

"I am a vegetarian," I reminded Sidney. "I had hoped there was some lemon meringue pie left."

"Get that bird out of my house." Having uttered a final time these cruel words, Sidney's mother disappeared from the head of the stairs. The sound of her door slamming followed.

"Let's all have lemon pie," George Morton suggested.

The next half hour was a difficult one for me. As we ate our pie, George kept after me to say certain words. He seemed to derive great enjoyment from hearing me repeat after him long and, as he must have thought, difficult words. Prestidigitation. Hegemony. Effervescence. Dichlorodiphenyltrichloroethane. It shames me to recall how willingly I performed for him. No doubt I found the stimulus of praise and applause irresistible. Sidney had never shown the least surprise at anything I did. There was no reason why he should. But his father seemed to think there was something remarkable in my repeating words after him. I blush to recall that I stopped all this by standing on the kitchen table and reciting the Gettysburg Address.

"A duck that talks," George said wonderingly when I was through. I could see that Sidney found my showing off disgusting.

"He's not a duck, Dad."

"Where did you get him?"

"From an Easter egg."

"Aw, come on."

"It's true. Isn't it true, Dormer?"

"So far as I know."

"If he's not a duck, what is he?"

"Perhaps I'm a prince on whom a wicked witch has cast a spell."

Sidney made a naughty noise. "He's been reading all those kid books."

"I'd say he's a duck," George said.

It was his last word on the matter. Sidney took me up to his room. Away from his father, he had nothing to say to me. I gathered that he was unhappy. He yawned and fell into bed.

"Turn off the light," he grumbled.

"I want to read."

"Then read in the closet with the door closed. I can't sleep with that light in my eyes."

Quick as a Dodo

It had never bothered him before when I read far into the night. I sensed that a first chapter of my life was drawing to a close. I took the dictionary with me into the closet and shut the door. Sidney always told me to "look it up" when I pestered him with questions. I wondered if I could look myself up in the dictionary. An urgent question pressed upon me as a result of the night's events: Who am I? What am I? What sort of bird can I be?

2

Look It Up

My intention was to see what the dictionary said of ducks, but as I turned the pages in search of that word my eye fell on another entry.

Quick as a Dodo

The picture, while inaccurate in several details, was nonetheless a reasonable likeness of myself.

You can imagine the emotion with which I read the words that follow.

> **do.do** (do/do), *n.*, *pl.* -DOES, DOS.
> 1. a clumsy, flightless bird of the genera Raphus and Pezophaps, about the size of a goose, related to the pigeons, formerly inhabiting the islands of Mauritius, Réunion and Rodriguez, but extinct since the advent of European settlers. 2. *Colloq.*, an old fogey. [Pg. *doudo*, prop., silly.]

Reading this in Sidney's closet by the light of a forty-watt bulb, I did not at first believe my eyes. I read the entry again. Ignoring for the moment the more tendentious and insulting aspects of that entry—clumsy and flightless indeed, and since when have the Portuguese earned the right to call others silly?—how could I possibly be a member of an extinct species? If I was alive, as indisputably I was, the species could not be extinct. On the other hand, if I was indeed a dodo, was I perhaps the only one, and if so, what did that portend for my own future and the future of the race?

I confess that I felt profound shame at the thought that I was a dodo. A species that has become extinct, so Darwin would have us believe, is possessed of some evolutionary flaw, incapable of surviving in altered circumstances. Had my ancestors simply withered and died with the advent of the settlers? But if there be guilt here, why pour it on the innocent dodo rather than on those Europeans?

When I turned off the light and snuggled into my slipper, I could not sleep. My mind kept turning to other dictionary entries, those devoted to Mauritius and Réunion. Both islands were described as "East of Madagascar." It was a phrase whose resonance I liked.

It had the sound of an old movie title, suggesting the romantic and the sinister, the unknown. Did the words stir up in me some atavistic memory of my origins? I tried unsuccessfully to visualize Mauritius and Réunion. It was nice to have a choice of a French or British native land. Of course, these islands are no longer colonial possessions; dictionaries, like atlases, go out of date swiftly nowadays, but Mauritius would have been a British possession and Réunion French in the time of my ancestors.

I cannot take responsibility for the banal character of my dreams. Against my closed lids formed an island no more realistic than an animated cartoon. It rose from a flat and monochrome sea, its sandy beaches giving way to verdure and vegetation, to palm trees, and, ultimately, to the volcanic mountain in the center of the island, whose cone wore a single halo of cloud as if it were blowing smoke rings at the impossibly blue sky.

Walking gracefully along the beach—without a trace of clumsiness, and one could see that he was anything but flightless, he simply preferred walking—was a dodo, a dodo undoubtedly myself.

I think this was the first dream in which I had cast myself as hero. My mission? I had returned to my native soil in order to lift others of my kind from the obscurity into which they had unjustly fallen.

The claim that our species is extinct was a vicious rumor floated by disgruntled colonists, angry at their inability to subjugate such a proud and noble bird. We had, it is true, been driven into the interior; we had unwittingly conspired in gaining credence for the rumor of our extinction. But what a civilization we had built in the interior of Rodriguez where no human had ever set foot!

I awakened smiling. My heart beat with pride. I was on my way to becoming a chauvinist dodo. My pride was tempered by further consultation of the dictionary. The genera Raphus—lovely word—and Pezophaps had been denied individual entry to the lexicon I used, so I turned to goose, then pigeon. It was good to know that I had relatives in adjacent species even if it should prove that I was the solitary dodo on the earth. Anger rose in me as my eye scanned the fourth entry for goose:

4. a silly or foolish person; a simpleton.

Such slander, perpetrated in the neutral tones of a dictionary, had a maddeningly unanswerable tone to it. The third meaning of pigeon continued the attack:

3. *Slang,* a simpleton, dupe, or gull.

Gull? Was there no limit to the ornithological calumny of this lexicographer?

I turned off the light again. I lay in the dark and seethed. A sense of obligation gathered in my breast. I had a duty to my species, but it extended as well to the genus or genera that contained, or had once contained, the dodo. Our collective good name must be vindicated. Why must I accept my lot as a domesticated, web-footed bird of the family Morton? I would leave the house. I would set forth into the world. I would discover for myself whether or not the dodo was an extinct species with the single exception of my humble self. No, not humble. Proud. I was a dodo and unafraid to say so. Flightless? More libel. I left the closet and went unclumsily downstairs. Dawn was breaking over the dewy lawn. In the trees, relatives were beginning to greet the sun with sleepy initial peeps and chirps. It seemed an auspicious moment for my first flight.

I began to run rapidly toward the back of the yard, unfolding my wings as I did so. Having

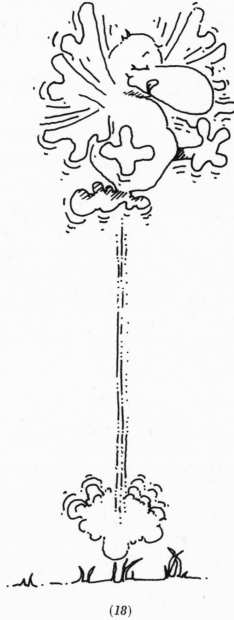

(*18*)

gained a certain momentum, I began to flap my wings, too rapidly at first, but I could feel the resisting air lift me. More surely, I pressed down against it and, marvelous sensation, began to rise. I cleared the back fence, but just barely, grazing a pointed picket with my foot. I was airborne. I was free.

No need to bore you with the details of that

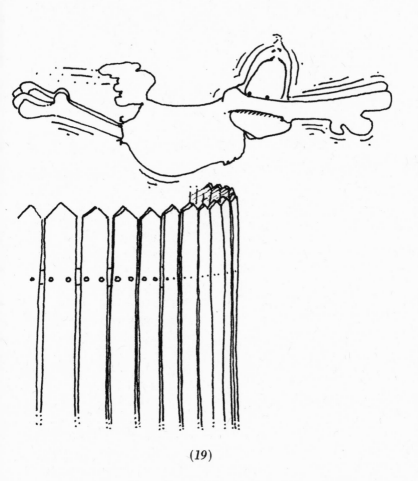

first exhilarating flight into the welcoming air. Suffice it to say that I stunted without stint. I did the loop the loop, I glided, I divebombed. I achieved total confidence in my abilities. I grew careless. As I skimmed across the Morton yard, I aimed for a particularly attractive stretch of sky. Unfortunately, it was sky reflected in the picture window. I hit with a great bang. I fell unconscious to the ground.

3

Mr. Cheeps

When I regained consciousness, a bearded man was looking down at me through rather thick glasses.

"Feeling all right?" he asked.

"Where am I?"

"I am Dr. Sundheit. I thought you were dead as a dodo when they brought you in here."

"Which dodo?"

"The dodo."

"Any dodo?"

He was puzzled. "Every dodo. There aren't any dodoes. That's the point."

"There, my friend, you are mistaken. I am a dodo."

His laugh revealed a number of gold fillings in his teeth. "And I am Peking Man," he said jovially enough.

Looking around me, I saw that I was in a white-walled, immaculately clean room. The table

I lay on was covered with black leather. Above
me, just over the shoulder of my chortling Pekin-
ese, was a very bright lamp, which, oddly, did
not hurt my eyes.

"Did Sidney bring me here?"

"No. Mr. Morton. He said he found you lying
unconscious beside the house. What happened?"

"Did I break anything?"

"Apparently not. No physical damage." He
shone a small penlight in my eye. "Still think
you're a dodo?"

Caution seemed indicated. I did not like the
way he asked the question. "What would you call
a bird who flies into a picture window?"

"So that's what happened. No wonder you
think you're a dodo."

"Oh, the pane. The pane."

"You're certainly not as dumb as a dodo. You
speak English beautifully. Mr. Morton must have
quite a way with animals." Mr. Morton appeared
in the doorway of the examining room. I found the
idea that George Morton had taught me anything
slightly hilarious, but that did not seem the moment to rob him of whatever borrowed glory my
fluency in English might have lent him. My initial
exchange with the doctor had prompted a new
line of thought, and one I knew instinctively it
would be best not to divulge either to Dr.
Sundheit or to George Morton. I kept my counsel
in the car going back to the house, but the drift of
my thought was roughly as follows.

I was a dodo. The dodo is thought to be an

extinct species. My troubled dreams of the night before had sought a source of pride and reassurance in the chance that I might discover other surviving dodoes and thus disprove the notion that we are extinct. Now, in the light of day, with my head clearing from the hard rap it had taken from the picture window, I began to see the advantages of my uniqueness.

Advantages of a logical sort, first of all. My banter with the doctor had made the point, admittedly in a jocular manner, that in my case there was no need to distinguish between the definite and indefinite articles, between *a* dodo and *the* dodo. I was not merely an individual of a given kind; I was an individual *and* a kind. No other creature could make that statement, unless Saint

Thomas Aquinas is correct and this is true of angels as well. The pride I felt in this status was far different from that I had derived from my dream of finding other dodoes somewhere east of Madagascar. The pride I now felt was close to vanity. Any bird is given to preening, but my new-found satisfaction with my condition went beyond that. I found that I *preferred* being the only surviving dodo. At that moment—and let my enemies make of it what they will—it would have grieved me deeply to come upon another dodo. I became aware of George Morton beside me. He had asked me a question, apparently several times.

"I beg your pardon."

He whistled with relief. "I thought you'd forgotten how."

"Forgotten how to what?"

"To talk. Say, you didn't speak to the vet, did you?"

"I answered his questions, yes."

Morton struck his forehead with his palm, making a slapping sound. This reawakened the ache in my own head. I had been going full tilt when I hit the picture window. I was lucky to be alive. The thought that I might have caused myself mortal injury, might actually have died, sent a tremor through me. It was borne in upon me that I had a special responsibility to take care of myself. I owed it to nature, to the world, to the Lord who had made me. When I went, a whole species would be wiped out. Here was a solemn thought indeed.

"Wasn't G.E. surprised?" Morton asked.

"The doctor? Sundheit thought I was lucky to have escaped physical injury."

"But how did he react when you spoke?"

Morton's expression was so pitiable that I could not refrain from telling him what the doctor had said.

"He was impressed by the way you have with animals."

"He thought I taught you English?"

"That seemed to be the point."

Morton could not meet my gaze but there was a silly smile on his face when he turned back to the road. "Well, well," he said.

However ridiculous I might find George Morton, it was unwise of me not to suspect that he could be dangerous too. I soon learned that fatuous self-satisfaction and insensitivity to the welfare of others go hand in hand. At the house, Morton took me to the sun porch where, before I knew what was happening, he had put me into a cage and locked it.

"There," he said in fruity tones. "Now you have a house of your very own."

This did render me speechless. I stared at him—through the bars!—and could not believe the benevolent smile he wore. Did he actually expect me to be grateful to him for locking me up in an absurd cage, one in which I could scarcely turn around? Morton, saying he would return, left the sun porch. I slumped to the floor of the cage, but not before I became aware of another cage in the room, not far distant from mine. Its occupant could only be Mrs. Morton's parakeet, who now studied me with beady eye.

"Where did they find you?" he asked haughtily.

"Please. I think I am going to cry."

"Whatever for? Don't you have water? Don't you have food?"

There was a cup of water and a dish of sunflower seeds imprisoned with me. Did Mr. Cheeps—for this was the parakeet's name—think that a cage was less a cage if it was well stocked with food? My thought went back to my first flight that morning, to the sense of freedom I had felt lifting above the earth and soaring aloft. Remembering that brief taste of liberty, I thought that my heart would break.

"Have you ever flown?" I asked Mr. Cheeps.

For answer, he fluttered about his cage, hopping from its floor to a small perch where he

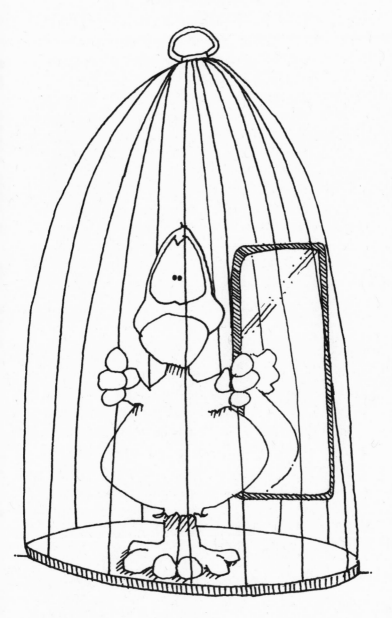

swung defiantly, and then began to hone his beak on the bars of his cage.

"I mean, really fly," I said. "Out of doors. High up into the sky."

Mr. Cheeps did not seem to understand.

"Don't you know that the world is full of free birds? They live in trees, in fields, everywhere. They can do whatever they wish. They sing and eat and fly."

"Wild birds," Mr. Cheeps said with disgust. "Yes, I've heard of them. Are you a wild bird?"

Could I honestly say what I was? I had been hatched beneath a pillow and until this morning had been sleeping in a slipper in Sidney's room. Did one flight into the outside world make me a wild bird? On the other hand, if Mr. Cheeps was typical, I was not a domesticated bird either. I had to escape. I would leave the Morton household and live among my kind. Well, among the cousins of my kind. I would seek out geese and pigeons. They would appreciate me. George Morton's notion of appreciation was to lock me up in a cage in the same room with an asinine parakeet. Mr. Cheeps was now engaged in pecking at a small bell attached to the bars of his cage, eliciting from it an insipid tinkle from which he seemed to derive great pleasure.

"Are you really content to live like this?" I asked.

"Like what?"

"The way you do. In that cage."

"It is all I have ever known."

"Poor bird. Haven't you ever craved companionship?"

"Mrs. Morton talks to me constantly."

"I meant the companionship of another bird."

"You are another bird. Now I have a companion."

"But I am not a parakeet."

"What is a parakeet?"

"You are a parakeet."

"I am Mr. Cheeps."

"I realize that. But there are many parakeets. Birds just like yourself."

"Nonsense."

"Do you think you are the only parakeet in the world?"

"Mrs. Morton assures me that I am."

Mr. Cheeps was impossible. I was furious at his assumption that our situations were identical. Did he really think he was unique? I turned away and spoke to him no more. After a time, he spoke to me, but I pretended that I did not understand him. Parakeet, as I had just proved, is a language easy to learn, even for someone who, like myself, finds whistling difficult. Now it served my purposes to have Mr. Cheeps think it escaped my powers entirely. Escape was more imperative than ever. The little parakeet summed up the ultimate danger. It was a chilling thought that a bird might come to love his prison.

4

Polly Want a Cracker

To be in a cage is one thing. To be seen in a cage is another. During the next several days, the sun porch at the Morton house might have been a miniature zoo with Mr. Cheeps and myself as the attractions, although I do not think it immodest to say that those who came there came to see me and not Mr. Cheeps. Whatever the proud and pampered parakeet might think, he was a dime a dozen; exact replicas of him could be purchased in stores throughout the nation. A dodo, on the other hand, even when it is not yet admitted that he is a dodo, is unlikely to be considered merely another bird. Of course, what drew visitors at first was George Morton's claim that I could talk.

"Keep your beak shut," Sidney advised. "Don't say a word. He'll get all these bigshots in to hear you talk and you just sit there."

"Dumb as a dodo?"

"Right!" Sidney laughed. It occurred to me that he was an unattractive child, untidy, overweight, unobservant. He leaned closer to the cage. "After all, I taught you to talk."

"Get me out of this cage, Sidney."

"It's locked."

"Unlock it."

"Dad's pretty mad about his slipper."

"You said it was an old one."

"He says it's the only pair his feet feel comfortable in."

"It was a privilege to fill his shoes," I said dryly. "Sidney, unlock this cage. Can you imagine what it's like being stuffed into a wire room? I can hardly turn around."

"Use your mirror." His grin seemed fiendish. Had I ever considered him a friend? There was, as it happens, a mirror in my cage. George Morton apparently thought I was a monkey. Still, I was able to put the mirror to scientific use. My profile, at least as much of it as I could see with only one mirror, indicated that I was a far more attractive creature than the dictionary illustration would lead one to suspect. Of course, the artist would have worked under the great disadvantage of never having seen what he was drawing. Perhaps he was a police artist, schooled in sketching suspects from the descriptions of their accusers. His picture of me would certainly make the grade as a poster. Wanted dead or alive? The world had had the dodo dead for quite some time. Was it ready for the dodo alive?

That first afternoon in the cage I became the blood brother of every parrot and minah bird in captivity. All those eager, taunting faces urging me to speak, telling me what to say, for all the world like George Morton over lemon meringue pie, only worse. Where had he found these people? When they addressed me, they spoke in what they assumed was a birdlike accent, their words prefaced by one squawk and ended by another. It was like Spanish punctuation. "Polly want a cracker." As God is my judge, this is what most of them wanted me to say. Perhaps I should not have been surprised. What does almost anyone say when asked to speak a few words into a tape recorder?

"Say it, Dormer," George Morton pleaded. His face, merely anxious at first, became a mask of embarrassment. "Dormer, Professor Sisson has come all the way from the university to see you. He is the most distinguished ornithologist in the state."

Sisson, a tall man with cranelike legs, the profile of a hawk, and something of that predator's unblinking look, stood staring at me in silence for five minutes. He ignored Morton's efforts to get me to demand a cracker in the name of Polly.

"First one I've ever seen," he said.

"Is he rare?" Morton asked. He seemed relieved to be distracted from my failure to speak.

"In this state he is unknown. Where did you get him?"

"My son found him on an Easter-egg hunt."

(*34*)

Sisson turned his startled gaze on George Morton. "The bird was hunting Easter eggs?"

"No. He was one of the eggs. Isn't that right, Sidney?"

Sidney, who had been standing beside his father, threw back his shoulders, closed his eyes, and began to speak in a high falsetto voice. "Last Easter in company with my companions I went hunting Easter eggs, as is the custom of the neighborhood. In the excitement, I was separated from the others and found myself alone in a small copse of trees. It was dark there, after the bright light of the sun, and I was scared. I feared that I was lost.

I sat down to get my bearings. The ground I sat on was soft and sandy. As I sat there, I began to dig in the sand, not thinking of what I was doing. And then I found this egg. It was very dirty, and at first I thought it was rotten, but after I spit on it and rubbed it a bit it looked okay, so I took it home and put it under my pillow where it hatched."

All this emerged as if on a single breath. It was clearly a recitation. It sounded like a lie from start to finish, and that had clearly been Sidney's intention. There was a long pause on the part of Professor Sisson. Finally he spoke.

"The egg was buried?"

"In sand."

"How deep?"

Sidney considered his arm. He indicated a point between the wrist and elbow.

"Measuring from the tips of your fingers?" Sisson took Sidney's hand and immediately let go, or tried to. As usual, Sidney's fingers were sticky with jam or candy. Sisson took out his handkerchief and rubbed his hand. "That would be about ten inches deep."

"I didn't know ducks bury their eggs," George Morton said.

"That's why they bury them," Sidney said.

"Duck?" Sisson said. "You think he's a duck?"

Sidney said, "He's an intransitive duck."

The lids of Sisson's eyes had lowered over those glistening orbs as he studied me more closely. "He puts me in mind of a mythical bird. The roc."

(*36*)

"That's how he flies," Sidney said, laughing in his odious way. "A roc in the picture window."

"I'll get you for that, Sidney. You'll be sorry."

"There!" George Morton cried. "Did you hear? He talked."

"Eh?" Professor Sisson said. "Eh?"

"Dormer spoke," George Morton shouted. "He just threatened my son." He was overjoyed.

Sisson's eyes were on Morton's lips, but he shook his head. He plucked a sort of plug from his ear and snapped it open. "Battery's gone dead," he observed. He had another with him. After the exchange was made, he smiled at Morton. "I thought you said this bird had just threatened your son."

"I did! He did! Do it again, Dormer."

I settled into my feathers, lifted my lids as if in sleep, and ignored them. The ornithologist made several indecisive remarks. He was obviously stumped by me and was finding it difficult to admit. George Morton continued to insist that I spoke English as well as anyone. Such faint praise was not calculated to stir me. And then genuine sleep overtook me.

5

Show Biz

In the marketplace of St. Denis, a century ago, an attractive female dodo might have been descried, moving among the stands, carrying a small wicker basket over which a protective cloth had been thrown. Who could mistake the glow of maternal love in her eye? Who could doubt the self-sacrifice of her mission? Otherwise distracted shoppers stepped aside for her, gentlemen of the old school gave her small deferential nods, here and there a planter flamboyantly snatched off his great hat as a sign of respect. It was common knowledge in St. Denis now. The dodo was doomed. In the language of a later day, the dodo was an endangered species, threatened not by natural disasters and the vagaries of evolution but by the folly of mankind. In my mother—for it was she who passed through that marketplace—they saluted a noble bird whose days were numbered. And then my mother saw what she had been look-ing for. It was a man. He wore the red pompom of the sailor, and his leathery look could only have been fashioned from many years at sea.

"Monsieur," my mother said, tugging at his sleeve. "Monsieur, a word with you."

In a quince the sailor's cap was in his hand. "Madame." He brought his heels together, but there was no resounding click. He was barefoot.

My mother locked her gaze with his. "I

should like to enlist your help in a scientific project of the gravest consequences."

"Madame?"

"Unless I am mistaken, you will soon set sail. You will be going far from this island. Is that right?"

"Madame is clairvoyant."

"Take this basket with you. Take it beyond the sea. Find a place that is secluded and sandy and warmed by the sun. And then . . ." She removed the cloth that covered the basket. The sailor leaned forward to look inside.

"*Sacre bleu,*" he cried, "*un oeuf!*"

"Precisely," my mother said. "An egg. My egg. You shall not see its like again. This is the future, Monsieur. I entrust it to you."

Tears were rolling from my eyes when I awoke. That noble, selfless woman. That trusted and trustworthy denizen of the deep. I was my mother's time capsule, her message to a later time, her defiance of destiny. I struggled to my webbed feet.

"Is he crying?" a voice asked.

"Perhaps the lights are too bright."

"We can't film without them."

"Will this be on tonight's news?"

"Unless something important comes up."

George Morton's face appeared among the glaring television lights. "Dormer," he said in urgent tones. "Dormer, the crew from the television station is here. They want to take some pictures. Do you understand? They have come to shoot some film of the talking duck. This is our chance, Dormer. Would you like to go on tour? Would you like to appear on 'Firing Line'? Then, speak, Dormer."

For a moment the solemnity with which George Morton spoke nearly melted my resistance. It was too reminiscent of my mother's voice in the dream from which I had just been rudely awakened. But then once more the polar ice cap descended upon the pulsing globe of my honest heart. I would not be an accomplice in his scheme to exploit me, certainly not for the wrong reason. A talking duck indeed.

A dissolute young man who seemed throttled by the paisley print ascot at his throat brought his face close to the cage and looked at me with a skeptical and bloodshot eye.

"Ugly duck, aren't you? Listen. No plugs, no profanity, no hello Mom or any of that. Do you have a prepared text?"

"He knows the Gettysburg Address," George Morton said.

"Uh uh. No you don't. Nothing controversial. Can he sing?"

"Sing! He talks. How many talking ducks have you met?"

"None so far. Say something, duck."

I sighed. "If 'twere done 'twere well 'twere done quickly. Is the camera running? Let's get this farce done with."

"Crazy. I like that." The director called over his shoulder. "Did you get that?"

From behind the lights, a voice informed him that they had recorded the words but the director's head blocked the view of the bird.

"Once more, baby," the director said and then was gone. A hush had fallen over the room. I became aware of a small red light piercing the larger glare. I addressed myself to it.

"I am the last dodo," I began quietly. "I am the living refutation of the belief that the dodo as a species is extinct. My current incarceration in this confining cage is only the latest atrocity perpetrated on my kind by the human race. I resent it deeply. Yet I do not ask compensatory damages. All I demand is my freedom. Uncage me. Release me. Let me fly again."

My voice rose with these last words. Admittedly, I was hamming it up, but in the end sincerity overwhelmed me. When I was done, the lights went down like stars dying in the morning sky. I blinked against the seeming darkness.

"Does he really think he's a dodo?" the director asked George Morton.

"Forget that. So he's crazy. He flew into a picture window this morning. But how about the voice, the accent, the delivery? I told you that duck could talk."

"I *am* a dodo," I insisted, but I was ignored.

"You better get an agent," the director advised Morton. "You could really clean up with that bird. But get him a writer. The dodo bit won't do." He turned and looked at me, but I was only an object for him, a thing. "I'd think about plastic surgery, too. Close-ups will murder him."

"Why did you talk?" Sidney asked accusingly. Elsewhere in the room the crew was gathering up equipment. Mr. Cheeps was singing his heart out in his cage, trying to get someone's attention, but in vain.

"Did you listen to what I said, Sidney?"

"Was that Dad's idea? Boy." Sidney shook his head in disgust.

A cunning plan occurred to me as I looked out at the sneer on Sidney's face. He was not hurt by my imagined disloyalty to him. He resented his father's small triumph as the champion of my elocutionary abilities.

"I'll make him rich," I sighed.

"Why would you do a thing like that?"

"Well, after all, in my hour of need he gave me the use of his slipper."

"He did not. I stole that slipper for you."

"Still, it was his slipper. I have incurred an obligation."

"What about me? I hatched you."

"That's true."

"I let you read half the night. I showed you where the refrigerator was. Is this the kind of thanks I get?"

"I hadn't thought of that."

"No, you forgot all that."

"But what can we do? My hands are tied."

"I don't know."

Stupid child. "If you unlocked this cage and let me out your father would be pretty disappointed. Of course you wouldn't do that. He owns me now."

"Who says I wouldn't? You just wait and see."

He left and I waited. When George Morton came to change the water in my cage he gave me a refill of sunflower seed, doubtless his way of expressing his thanks for what I had done for him.

"Good duck," he said, attempting to pat my bill. I turned away before contact was made. "Can I get you anything?"

"I'd like something to read," I confessed.

"Good Lord. Do you read too?"

"I prefer the dictionary for desultory reading."

"The dictionary! The duck who reads dictionaries." His eyes glazed. Did he see that legend up in lights?

The dictionary proved to be my salvation, and there is a moral here for you, my child. When George brought the book out to the sun porch even he could see that it would not fit inside my cage. He tried to prop it up outside my bars, but I shook my head.

"No good. I like to browse, just page around until something catches my eye. I'd like to sit in that rocking chair."

"That rocker?"

He considered this. He checked the windows in the room. Locked. The door could be locked from the outside. He stood with his arm on the mantle of the fireplace and thought some more.

"All right. We have to trust one another. You can read in the rocking chair. I'll make sure you're not disturbed."

"Maybe you could lock the door."

"Yes! Yes, I could do that. Then no one can get in."

"Or out," I said, chuckling.

"Ha ha," George Morton said.

Some minutes later, I was ensconced in the rocking chair with the dictionary in my lap. George Morton had gone, locking the door behind him. Mr. Cheeps stared at me from his swaying perch.

"Can you really read?"

"Only words."

My ear was straining to hear if George was

still outside the door. At the window, the afternoon sun was bright. I could see birds flitting about: several robins on the lawn, a cardinal at the feeder, sparrows everywhere.

I put down the dictionary and crossed the room to the fireplace. I stepped inside and looked up. As I had hoped, as I had prayed, a small rectangle of sky was visible at the top of the shaft. I withdrew my head and looked at Mr. Cheeps. It seemed appropriate to say something to record the significance of the moment. I was about to ascend that chimney like Saint Nick. Soon I would be on my own in a world I was learning to distrust.

"It is a far far better thing . . ." I began, then stopped. Mr. Cheeps had put his head beneath his wing and gone to sleep. Clearly this historic moment did not interest him. Sobeit. I turned and stepped back into the fireplace.

Just fly up and out, that was my idea, but I had no sooner gotten a good start than I was stopped by the snugness of the chimney. This was going to be a tight squeeze, perhaps too tight. And then, from below, echoing strangely, I heard the sound of George Morton's anxious voice.

"Dormer, you're off your rocker. Dormer." He actually began to whistle, as for a dog.

I pressed my feet against the sides of the chimney and boosted myself upward. If the chimney did not narrow more I might be able to make it.

"Where did he go, Mr. Cheeps?" Morton cried. "Where is he?"

That perfidious parakeet told everything he knew. Fortunately, he knew little and George Morton could not understand a word he said. I could hear furniture being overturned. I heard the windows fly up. I looked upward. The sky, freedom, seemed so near, but the passage was now so small that my feathers were pressed tightly against my body and it was difficult to move my legs. My wings were of course useless in that confined space. And then the voice of George Morton was loud beneath me.

"All right, Dormer. I see you. Come on down."

I gave a mighty boost and my bill cleared the chimney top. How vivifying the air of freedom was. I drank deep draughts of it. Another push and I was completely free of the chimney shaft. I steadied myself and looked down at the roof of the Morton house, outward at the lawn, to the street beyond. In the distance was a copse of trees. Was it there that I had been found?

The foreshortened figure of George Morton appeared on the front lawn. Sidney came out too and finally, Mrs. Morton. George pleaded with me to come down. I saw that he had the dictionary with him. He held it up to me as if it were bait. Sidney's expression was difficult to read. He was clearly enjoying the fact that his father's hopes were being thwarted but he did not appear to like it that I had effected my own escape. Mrs. Morton? She was shaking her apron at me and saying "Shoo."

I lifted my head then, ignoring them. My feathers were a mess from the chimney, but fluttering and preening them helped. I was conscious that my presence on the Morton chimney top was emblematic, a symbol of something I only imperfectly understood. I poised myself, gripping the chimney top with my feet. The slight breeze was strong in my nostrils. I flexed my legs, pushed off, and then, gloriously, wonderfully, I was aloft. I was flying. The whole expanse of sky was mine at last. I made a ceremonial pass over the Morton yard, a little nod in the direction of history, and then I climbed steadily, rejoicing in the liberating lilt of flight. But I kept one eye cocked on that copse of woods where the strangest egg of all had been unearthed.

6

My Cousins the Pigeons

After a looping, leisurely flight to the south—
my intention was to mislead the Mortons
as to my destination, but I no longer seriously en-
tertained fears that they could recapture me—I
returned, flying at treetop level. I passed over a
playing field and then approached from the south
the copse of trees I had come to identify as the
place where, according to one of his accounts, Sidney had found me on that fateful Easter-egg hunt.
I circled it several times, but the trees were in full
leaf now, and it was impossible to see what kind of
terrain lay below them. I had watched other birds
landing in and taking off from trees, but some
instinct told me that such antics were not for the
dodo. The dodo can land only on land. On water
too, to be sure, but my short flight had revealed no
pond or lake or stream. Another instinct caused me
to regret this.

A final circle around the copse of trees and

then I came in low and touched down under a tall pine at the edge of the stand. Beneath the carpet of needles was indeed a sandy soil. Questions crowded one upon the other in my mind.

How did the erstwhile egg I was find its way to this unlikely landbound spot? My dream of a French sailor might have been a revelation of sorts, a message encoded long ago during the journey from that island east of Madagascar. Or could it have been my mother herself? I had read of the heroic feats mothers perform in moments of emergency, the adrenalin miraculously conferring on them abilities they would lack at any other time. Had my mother undertaken the long flight from the Indian Ocean to the land of the free and the home of the brave? I formed an image of her, breasting the air currents as she winged her way westward across the sea, desperation in her movements, determination in her eye. She was making her last flight, a flight of supreme importance, so that she might lay a final egg in a place where her young had a chance of survival. We know little of the habits of dodoes. How do they nest? How do they hatch their eggs? How long does it take? Doubtless, if I had been a female dodo all this knowledge would have been mine instinctively. As it was, I had only my imagination and my extraordinarily keen mind. It was my imagination that suddenly delivered up another possibility that gave me pause.

If one egg, why not more? The dodo would be a far more singular bird than it undoubtedly is if it did not lay several eggs at once. Whoever had hidden me here might have hidden other eggs as well. I looked about me, conscious of the beating of my heart. Was it possible that potential brothers and sisters now lay about me, hidden in the sand, still awaiting the discovery and release that had come to me?

I began to walk about under those trees. I was in search of some sign of the digging that had taken place last Easter when I had been uncovered. Indians, we are told, can read the ground as if it were a palimpsest, one story written upon another, history in a broken twig, the turn of a leaf, a disturbance in the soil. I was no Indian. The ground looked much the same everywhere I looked. Engrossed in my search, I was at first only faintly aware of voices and paid them no mind until finally they registered, and the fear that humans were near gripped me. It was a measure of my fear that I did not at once think to rise into the air and fly to safety.

The voices came closer. Blood beat like drums in my ears, doubtless impairing my hearing. I gasped for air and looked wildly about me. I saw the pigeons before I associated the chatter I had been hearing with them. And then relief caused me to cry out. The talking stopped. A dozen pairs of eyes were trained on me.

"Hello," I called, mimicking the language they had been speaking. "Welcome to these woods."

A very plump pigeon separated himself from

the others and moved jerkily toward me, his head cocked to the side, one watchful eye on me. He stopped a short distance away.

"What was that you said?" His voice burbled forth and his chest seemed to inflate as he stood there.

"I said hello. Hello and welcome."

"But we live here. Who are you?"

"My name is Dormer."

"You're not a pigeon."

"Not exactly, no."

"There are no inexact pigeons. Either one is a pigeon or one is not."

"I am not. I am a dodo."

"You needn't be offensive."

"I have no intention of being offensive. I am a

(54)

dodo. A dodo is a distant relative of the pigeon. We are, in a manner of speaking, cousins."

The other pigeons came closer now, surrounding me, though not in a menacing way. The pigeon, even in numbers, is not a menacing bird.

"My name is Green," the pigeon who had first approached me said.

"How odd."

"Why do you say that?"

"Because you're gray."

"On the contrary, I am green."

"And I am Purple," another said. "My name is Fuchsia," said a third. And then they all chirped in. There names were Orange and Aqua and Russet and Ebony, and so on. And every blessed one of them was silver gray.

Green came close to me and whispered, "Don't say anything. The others are color blind."

The others? But of course they all were, Green included. I asked him what he thought of my color.

"I have never been partial to yellow," he said, "but then you didn't choose your color."

"No, I didn't." My color verges on umber.

Green turned to the others. "This goose is our friend. He says his name is . . ." He turned to me.

"Dormer."

"Dormer. I shall call him Yellow, because of his color."

"But he's maroon," Purple protested, even as Aqua insisted that I was white.

"Silence," Green boomed and his chest expanded mightily. "We will call him by his own name. Dormer. Dormer is the word in his language for the color he is."

This brought gurgling agreement from the flock. They crowded around me, bumping against me, cooing in a friendly fashion. A lump formed in my throat. For the first time in my life I had gained acceptance and affection from beings of roughly the same kind as myself. It was a tender moment, never to be forgotten. Oh, it is all very well to talk of the struggle of life, of the survival of the fittest, of nature red in tooth and claw. Nonetheless, in the long run, what we crave and need is affection and love.

7

The Invention of DO

Those pigeons made me feel welcome, truly one of the flock. Whatever they did enthralled me, and I approved of their every custom. At first. With familiarity, the critical sense awoke, and it was difficult to ignore the fact that much of what the pigeons did was wanting in rhyme and reason. This was particularly noticeable in matters of exchange. Let me explain.

One morning I noticed Purple giving Aqua some kernels of corn in exchange for a tattered ribbon. Purple then traded the ribbon to Orange for a stale piece of bread which he took to Ebony for a berry Ebony said was blue and Purple thought was green. Actually, the berry was red, but that is not my point. In order to get that berry, Purple had had to engage in a lengthy trading process. These pigeons were desperately in need of a monetary system, and I set about devising one for them.

The first step, of course, was to have a common medium of exchange, some item with reference to which all other goods might be compared. Needles fallen from the trees were too plentiful, but pine cones commended themselves. I gathered together all the fallen cones, reflecting that it was appropriate that they grew on trees. I called the pigeons together and they formed a circle around me.

"Friends," I said. "I want to teach you a new game. We will call it DO. You see these cones. They are not cones. They are DO. I am going to distribute them among you."

I dealt them until each pigeon had an equal amount.

"The DO you now have is a precious commodity. Purple, you have a berry I want. I will give you two DO for it."

"What is two?"

"Don't you know numbers?"

They all shook their heads. I gave Purple one cone. Then I gave him another. I pointed with my bill, saying as I did so, "DO.DO."

"Dodo," Purple repeated. I took the berry.

I went to Aqua and put a cone in front of him. "I will give you that for a kernel of corn."

The sale was made. The principle was grasped, and soon the little group was busily engaged in trade. I had never seen them happier. I myself was saddened because they had no numbers. This was particularly astonishing because they had the English alphabet. I decided to fashion a system of calculation, using letters as the Greeks had done.

You will recall that my basic monetary unit was DO. You will further perceive, as the pigeons did not, that I had named the system after myself, a pardonable piece of vanity, I think. After all, remember the watt, the ampere, the lynch, and the gerrymander. Very well, the basic unit being DO, I needed techniques of multiplication and division employing letters.

When a letter prefixes the basic unit, this has the effect of multiplying DO by the number the letter has in the alphabet, beginning the count with 2, the first number in the classical sense. Thus:

aDO = DO + DO (2 DO, as we should say)

bDO = DO + DO + DO (that is, 3 DO)

And so on. When a letter is added to DO, this has the effect of dividing the basic unit.

DOa = one half DO
DOb = one third DO

And so on. With these simple matters in hand, my

pigeons fell to elementary calculation with even more gusto than they had shown for trade. The following equations were quickly established:

$$aDO = (DOa + DOa) + (DOa + DOa)$$
$$DO = DOa + (DOc + DOc)$$

Others, equally obvious, followed. It was time to assign exercises.

Exercise 1

1. A pigeon from Peoria is flying east with pDO to see Purdue play Notre Dame. The ticket costs DO, food and lodging cDO, and a present for Mom bDO. How much does the pigeon have on returning to Peoria?

2. A pigeon in Newark has DOb; his cousin in Miami bDO. Each inherits gDO. How much DO does the Miami cousin have *if* it costs him bDO to go north to claim his inheritance?

It is said that there is a little larceny in everyone. There is also a little teacher, very little in most cases, but surely some. What a pleasure it is to see in the eyes of the pupil that sudden dilation signifying understanding. Nonetheless, there came a time when I regretted having invented DO

Green and Purple proved to be particularly smitten by DO, or rather the theory of DO. Prodded by them, I introduced further refinements into the system, notably the addition of multiple prefixes and suffixes. The next step was to introduce expressions including both a prefix and suffix. The floodgates were opened when Green and Purple insisted that I admit multiple prefixes and multiple suffixes. I had a premonition that this was unwise, but I had no desire to stand in the path of pure reason. More exercises were demanded.

Exercise 2

1. How much DO is DOpe worth?
2. How much is that DOggy in the window?

Child's play.

Exercise 3

1. Express unDO otherwise.
2. How much DO did the pigeon who made a toDO make?
3. Give alternative expressions of abDOmen.
4. After a flyer in the market, a pigeon found himself with conDOr. State in another way how much DO he had.

Imagine the scene there in that copse of trees. Everywhere pigeons were brushing away pine needles and working more and more elaborate formulations in the sand. Most of the pigeons ob-

served moderation in playing DO, but some, notably Green and Purple, seemed unable to get their fill. Others might turn with relief to amassing or spending DO, but Green and Purple no sooner finished one exercise than they demanded another. I obliged them, but with foreboding. At meals, their conversation was a vexation.

"What part of a DO is a DOzen?" Green would snap.

"How much DO is a DOllar?" Purple would counter.

They had acquired the knack of working these comparatively simple problems in their heads, but they demanded complete silence while they did so. This had a depressing effect on the community meal.

"You must stop doing this," I suggested gently to Green.

"DOing," he said, puffing his chest and closing his eyes. He began to calculate.

"No. No. Green, I admire your interest. I respect your mind. But you are undoubtedly . . ."

"UnDOubtedly," he cried.

"Stop it. Please." I turned to his companion in calculation. "Purple, have you two completely lost your taste for indolence?"

"InDOlence," Purple repeated. "Give me a minute now. I'll get it."

8

The Morality of DO-ing

I reported my failure to the others, leaving Green and Purple to their calculations. Someone grumbled that he wished that I had never introduced DO among them. It was difficult not to agree, or at least to sympathize with the thought.

"It is too late now," I said. "Once DO has been introduced into a society, there is no going back. The problem is not to eliminate it, but to control it."

"How?"

"By government," I said. "The rules of DO are one thing. But the rules for playing DO are something else."

"I don't understand," Aqua said.

"The point is a simple one," I said, "though there does not seem to be a simple way of expressing it. Take a problem in DO. For example, how much less than one DO is DOuble? There are rules for arriving at the right answer."

They all agreed somewhat impatiently.

"Now imagine yourself grappling with that problem while beside you a fellow pigeon writhes in pain, his foot caught beneath a stone that he is unable to lift by himself. You continue working on your DO problem. You solve it. Your solution is correct by the rules of DO. Nonetheless, you have not done well."

There was a chorus of assenting coos.

"You have broken no rule of DO, but you have not done well. If I should say that you have broken a rule for *playing* DO, I would not mean to restrict these rules to when and how and where DO may be played. These are rules which must guide us from morn to night, whether we are playing DO or doing something else."

"Moral rules," Quartz, a grizzled old pigeon, said.

"Precisely. Unlike the rules of DO, moral rules are rules that you all already know. If I should state such a rule, you would know immediately that you had always known it."

"Give an example," Aqua urged.

"A pigeon must never ignore another pigeon in distress."

Their coos indicated agreement.

"Never treat a pigeon in a way you would not want to be treated yourself."

The reader will see where I was leading my little flock. They saw now that they were already in possession of rules that took precedence over the rules of DO. What was not yet clear to them was the need for enforcement of these moral rules. If every pigeon knows the moral rules, not every pigeon abides by them in every instance. What then? Punitive sanctions were in the offing, to be imposed either by the whole flock or by someone acting in their name. That is, these pigeons were about to take another step away from innocence. Government was next.

I did not have it in me to continue the discussion then. I felt weary. I felt as missionaries must have felt when first they set foot on those islands east of Madagascar, bearing the burden of the truth. It is a terrible responsibility to awaken in others the knowledge of good and evil, even in such welcoming lodgement as the pigeon breast. I wanted to be by myself for a time. Precipitation was not the order of the day, though it had grown cloudy. I set off down a little-used path and Aqua accompanied me part way.

"You have brought interesting things into our lives, Dormer."

"You have given me friendship. You have given me a home."

I sensed that these pigeons were liable to grant me more importance than I deserved. Naturally, I felt superior to them. After all, I was a dodo. If I now introduced the concept of government, was it not inevitable that I should become their leader? *Il Duce* the dodo. I was both exhilarated and depressed by the prospect. Eminence attracts, but this side of the Rubicon? The truth was my ambition unleashed would range beyond this copse of trees and my simple cousins.

Aqua left me, scuffling off among the trees, erasing as he went some old DO calculations. I could hear the half-mad voices of Green and Purple urging one another on. Faster music, stronger wine, more difficult problems. "DOdecanese" Purple cried, and "PapaDOpoulos," Green replied. Their single-minded pursuit of knowledge depressed me mightily, and my mind turned to basic questions. What had brought me here? What indeed? I had half forgotten that I was the last of the dodoes, that I had come to this copse of trees because it was here that Sidney had found the egg I had been. And an earlier question returned.

Was it possible that there were other dodo eggs buried here? Had I, while playing teacher to the pigeons, been delaying the birth of my siblings?

I stopped on the path. Actually the path had stopped too. I was in a less-frequented part of the copse. It was cool there and quiet. The cooing of pigeons was no longer audible, and I realized that this was a relief to me. I had need of solitude. And of rest.

I made a nest of pine needles under a great

tree whose branches seemed to extend over me in benediction. Snuggling my bill into my feathers, I made a blank of my mind and was soon asleep.

I Become a Father

How long I slept I do not know. When I awoke it was dark. Voices were audible. My name was being called. The pigeons. My pigeons. But something had broken the sympathetic link I had left with them. To go back would be to go back to power and responsibility. Was it for that, that a member of a supposedly extinct species had been preserved? As if to make myself less visible, I shifted and wiggled my body, sinking more deeply into the little nest I had improvised for my nap. I seemed to have constructed it over a depression, since my efforts had a marvelous effect. I seemed to be working myself into the very ground, sandy as it was. And then I felt against my bosom a resistant object. It felt like a stone, and I brushed aside the pine needles in order to eject it from my nest. The light, as I have said, was poor, but when the needles were removed, the object uncovered no longer appeared to be a stone. For a moment I kept my mind free of thought as if fearful to admit the idea, but then, with joy, with thanksgiving, I said the word aloud, hardly more than a whisper, and there was a reverence in my voice that brought tears to my eyes.

"An egg," I said. "An egg!"

This was a dodo egg. I was completely and totally certain of it. Everything indicated the truth of the supposition. This was the copse where Sidney had found me. I had come here looking for other dodo eggs. Distracted for a time, I had now turned my mind again to my reason for being. And *voilà,* an egg. Of course it was a dodo egg. It had to be.

The voices of the pigeons were closer now. How urgent the sound of my name cried out in the gloaming! Those pigeons might have been staving off their fear of the impending dark by calling me.

I felt an impulse to answer, but the smooth round pressure of the egg against me kept me silent. That egg represented a far more imposing obligation than the pleas of my cousins the pigeons.

As despair increased in the voices of the pigeons, hope rose in my own breast, pressed against the shell of the egg that encased another like myself. A brother? A sister? It did not matter. One of my own. I was alone in the dark now, yet not alone. Hunger and thirst joined me there in the nest, but I had no intention of leaving the egg, not even for an instant. Even if it took days, a week, more, I was intent on remaining where I was, warming the egg, coaxing its occupant to stir, to kick, to break the shell and come forth into the world. If one dodo is good—and who could doubt it?—two dodoes would be better still.

It is not given to many males to dream the dreams of a mother, but such were my dreams, as I sat on that nest covering the egg, that they would not have been unworthy, perhaps, of a mother. Of my own mother, even, whose egg I was convinced this was. Instinctively I had put myself at the service of this egg, of the future, of the race. How liberating it was to be tugged away from considerations of *my* good, of what was beneficial to *me*. The wider perspective that included this egg as well was welcome.

I intended now to live for my kind, for our common good. No longer would "to be Dormer" and "to be a dodo" be logically equivalent. No expectant mother has listened more alertly than did

I for the first stir of life in the egg I warmed. My sleep was fitful, for when it came it was interrupted by what seemed movement in the egg beneath me. Groggy, hungry, my thirst unslaked, I was plagued by dreams that seemingly occurred in the passage between sleeping and waking. Noises heard in my dreams sounded as if from the real world. How often I was certain that my long vigil was over and the egg about to hatch, only to realize that it was only in my head that stirrings had occurred.

The second night it rained, hard, and I was able to slake my thirst and snack on some edible algae that appeared in the pool that formed beside my nest. That seemed a good omen. I need not risk leaving my egg in order to forage for food. Would my resolution to remain on that egg until it hatched have been so firm if I had known it would take more than a week? The days seemed to lengthen; my nights of desultory sleep did not refresh me. Toward the end I was reduced to working ever more complicated problems in DO.

I must have been almost as mad as Green and Purple when respite came in the form of an undeniable sound from the egg. I lifted up, not trusting my ears, but the sound repeated itself. The egg appeared actually to move. Lowering myself once more, I found the temptation strong to mimic the trumpeter swan and send a triumphant call through the copse of trees.

The end of my ordeal was more than compensation for the long days and nights. I lay there listening to the sounds of scuffling within the shell. Might I not have given the little tyke a hand, breaking the shell with my own bill? How I wanted to do this, but I was resolved that nature, having gone into abeyance for a century, should now pursue her own course. Besides, I was alarmed. The fragility of life, the ease with which any living thing might not have been any living thing—not only the dodo—filled me with awe, and I understood the prayer which forms on a mother's lips, a prayer of thanksgiving, but principally a prayer of praise. What an extraordinary universe it is when contemplated from the inside, as it were, when one is involved in its mysterious workings and not occupying some imaginary vantage point outside.

The time came when I had to get off the nest. No further aid was required of me. The rest was up to the squirm and kick of that little creature. Attempting to stand, I staggered. I was weak with hunger and stiff from inactivity. I ate a hurried breakfast not far from the nest, my eye never leaving it, and then, restored, I took up my vigil again.

The egg rocked and rolled now with the efforts of its occupant. The first crack appeared, it widened, then closed. More motion inside and once more the crack began to open. A head forced its way into the light.

A small head. A prehistoric head. A head and then a neck that seemed covered with armorial skin. Apparently the dodo head needs time to assume its distinctive and attractive shape. My kinsman, his nose in the world, seemed to pause for rest. His eyes of course were closed. I had yet to look deeply into the gaze of a fellow dodo. The head moved, trying the air, drinking it in. My heart beat in the presence of this new citizen of the world. The second dodo in more than a century had put in his appearance.

With renewed effort, the little devil freed himself from the shell. It fell apart. I stepped back. What manner of body was this? No wings were visible. I was prepared for two legs, but four? And then it began to move. Slowly, very slowly. A ray of sunlight fell upon it. My breathing had stopped. There was no mistaking now what it was I had given birth to. The new creature moved again. Again I stepped back, making room for the baby turtle that crept blindly over the earth as if still scaling the inner walls of its egg.

10

One of a Kind

I flew away. I stumbled into the air, beating my wings in anger and frustration. I rose almost perpendicularly through the trees into the air above, and I continued to climb. I might have been on my way to make a protest to the maker of us all. The air thinned and my chest hurt and an ache began behind my eyes, but still I flew upward. And then I blacked out.

It is a startling thing to regain consciousness while engaged in a nosedive. The wind roared in my ears, I accelerated as I dropped, my wings flat against my body, limp. With an effort, I got them open, braking my fall and then gradually altering it to a long, swooping descent. To cut my speed, I circled the copse of trees three times, gliding, and then came in for a landing at the point from which I had taken off. The newborn turtle had moved four inches in my absence. With what mixed emotions I looked at the awkward beast I cannot say.

And yet, after all, was it his fault he was not a dodo? What blame could he be made to bear for the hopes with which I had hatched him? That it was I who had hatched him was a marvel that had not diminished, despite my disappointment.

I was responsible for this beast. His egg, like my own earlier, had been doomed, except for the caprice of accidental discovery. Well, unlike Sidney, I took a stern view of the responsibility I had taken on by fathering this turtle. Fathering. But, if I was a father, this was my son, struggling blindly across the earth. He had shuffled off one shell, but he was still contained by another. I got down on the ground beside him.

"Son," I said, and I confess that my voice broke. "Son."

His imperceptible movement stopped. He turned his head towards me; it was rough hewn, all planes, canvas stretched over a frame, a miniature dinosaur's head. And then his eyes opened and he was looking at me. I was the first thing he

saw in this world. I decided that he was the next best thing to a dodo. He nuzzled my cheek and made a small mewling sound. Good grief, he must be hungry. But what do turtles eat? Turtle food, of course. But in what does that consist? How I longed to have a minute or two in the Morton house where I might have consulted *World Book* and briefed myself on turtles.

As I stood there, perplexed, Green came walking out of the woods.

Green had changed greatly since I had last seen him, and changed for the worse. He had a ravaged look. His feathers were disheveled and unclean, and there was a glint in his eye that made me slightly nervous. Although he was walking straight toward me and my son, he seemed unaware of this. Assuming that he would take note of us sooner or later, I waited, but then, seeing that he did not mean to stop, that he was about to step on my son, I gave him a push, upsetting him. He looked at me, surprised.

"Why hello, Dormer." The glint came back in his eye. "DOrmer! Let me see."

"Stop!" I cried. "Do you realize that you nearly stepped on my son?"

"Your son? Where is he?"

"There."

"He looks like a turtle."

"He is a turtle."

"Strange."

"What do you mean?" I asked, irked.

"A violet turtle. But perhaps his mother is violet?"

"I've never met her."

Green closed one eye and looked at me with

the other. "Are you entered in any of the contests?"

"I know nothing of any contests."

"The annual animal contests. Everyone takes part. It's a magnificent affair."

Whatever these contests might be, Green's mention of them seemed to restore some of his former good sense. When he suggested that we get back to the others, as if I had just left a minute before, I saw no reason not to accompany him. I put my son on my back, and we set off up the path toward home.

"What is your son's name?" Green asked.

"Otto."

"Isn't he mobile?"

When I got back to the pigeon flock some of the trepidation I had felt in returning to them dissipating, I learned that DO had fallen into such low repute among them, because of the excesses of Green and Purple, that it was for all practical purposes a forgotten pastime. I noticed piles of abandoned pine cones lying here and there about the clearing. It was just as well. If barter is time consuming, it is also a good way to meet lots of people. I got Aqua aside and asked him about the contests Green had mentioned.

"There's a turtle on your back."

"Yes, I know. Has Green invented these contests?"

"They were held long before Green was born. Would you like me to remove the turtle?"

"Certainly not. He's my son."

"Ha ha. Then he is a dodo too, I suppose."

"Of course not. He's a turtle."

"Then you must be a turtle too. A turtle dove perhaps."

"Tell me about the contests."

"Are you a turtle?"

"Would it make any difference if I were?"

"It certainly would. You could enter the turtle race."

"I may enter my son."

"You won't be able to carry him then."

"He will need no help from me. For his age, he is extremely swift. There are turtles in the races then, not just pigeons?"

"There is one of each in each contest. That is the point of them. The whole animal kingdom, at least those species of it that live in this state, gathers annually for the event."

"Are you entered?"

"I am in the aqua-colored pigeon relay race."

"I see. How did you do last year?"

"I won."

"Congratulations."

"Oh, I win every year."

"Well, well. I had no idea you were such an athlete."

What little interest I had in the contests waned when I took Otto off my back and let him crawl about on his own. The pigeons were fascinated by him and came to watch him move about. I shooed them away. I wanted to be alone with my son. I sought privacy some distance from the pigeons who went back to their exercising, getting ready for the contests, whatever exactly they were.

Otto looked at me with lidded eyes and I had the strange sensation of being observed from a prehistoric time. "Dada," he said.

"No," I corrected. "Dodo."

"Dada dodo."

"Correct. And you are a turtle. There are things I must tell you of the world, Otto, since you entered it largely because of me. Our kinship consists in the fact that the eggs that bore us were buried against a future that must have seemed obscure and perilous to our parents. Providence,

luck, the vagaries of chance, conspired to make that future a reality. Life is a mystery, Otto. However unlikely our own entry into it might have been, our status is really not much different from the common status of creatures. Have you any idea of the statistical improbability of any living thing's being born?"

Otto blinked and said nothing, but I could see that I had his full attention.

"I am a dodo," I said unctuously. "I know that this may seem incredible to you. It continues to amaze me. I am, as matters stand, one of a kind. This cannot be said of you, Otto, at least not in the same sense. But you must not repine."

Otto's eyes drifted over my shoulder. A quizzical expression formed on his ancient newborn face. Perhaps I had reached the limit of his attention span. I glanced in the direction he looked. An extremely large turtle was lumbering across the clearing. I got to my feet.

"That is not your son," the turtle said when it had drawn near.

"Sir," I began.

"Madam," she corrected. "You have kidnapped my child. You have robbed my nest and made off with my offspring."

"Your offspring!" I laughed disdainfully. The word connoted an agility inapplicable to a turtle.

"My child."

"Otto, do you recognize this woman?"

Need I say that the cause was lost before the battle had even been joined? Little Otto crept close to the hulking form of the female turtle. I had lost a son but he had gained a mother. It would have been perverse to try to drive a wedge between them. Nature makes a formidable foe, and it was nature that had linked Otto and his mother. So I left them, mother and child, and

started toward the pigeons. Halfway across the clearing, I changed direction and went away behind a tree where, unashamedly, I wept.

Alone, alone. One of a kind. Never had my distinction seemed more of a tragic burden than it did at that moment. The world wavered and ran as

I looked about me with tear-filled eyes. I was conscious of someone joining me.

"I see that your wife has arrived," Aqua said.

"My wife?"

"The little one's mother."

"She is not my wife."

"Aha."

"I shall never have a wife," I said mournfully. "I am doomed to a life of celibacy. It is a bitter thing, Aqua, to be the last point on the line, the sole survivor of an extinct species."

"There are worse things than celibacy, Dormer."

"Don't mock me."

"Put your mind to other things. Think of the coming contests. There is much to divert you."

He meant well. Inadequate as his consolation was, it was good of him to make the effort. I assured him that I would lose myself in the contests. How often it is our half-hearted promises that we keep most faithfully.

11

Quick as a Dodo

Dawn broke on the long awaited day. The first rays of sunlight penetrated the pines and brought awake the beasts who throughout the night had been arriving in order to take part in the annual animal games. As I looked about me that bright morning, I felt that I was looking at half the cargo of the Ark. Aside from the pigeons and Otto and his mother, there was but one representative of each animal species: one rabbit, one fox, a variety of dogs but no two of the same breed: a frog, a toad, a bluejay, and on and on. The chorus of voices verged on cacophony. Excitement was palpable. After the most spartan of breakfasts, we all adjourned to the playing fields.

These consisted of the grounds of a high school whose students were now on vacation. I took a seat in the bleachers where I had a good view of the cinder track encircling the oval of the football field. The fact that so many events were to take place prevented one from seeing everything. As at a circus, one had to choose which ring to watch. But it was not this alone that bewildered me.

Directly before me a rabbit race was held. A single rabbit got on his mark, tensed his body, and waited for the gun. Bang, and the rabbit streaked down the track and breasted the tape to a great burst of applause. Moments later he mounted a little platform, bowed his head for the reception of the medal, then stood erect while some music was

played. More applause. This same sort of thing seemed to be occurring elsewhere on the field. I left my seat and sought after Aqua.

"There is only one contestant in each event," I said.

"Yes."

"He cannot lose."

"A winner is never a loser."

"Granted. But wouldn't it make more sense to have the contest decide who should be the winner?"

"No. It would be unfair."

"You mean that it would be unfair to have Otto, for example, race against the rabbit."

"Against Virgil? Yes indeed. But then it would be unfair to have Virgil race another rabbit. But what am I saying? It would not be unfair, it would be unintelligible."

"Please explain."

Aqua adopted a patient smile. "Imagine that two rabbits—we shall call them A and B—are entered in the same race."

"Good."

"The gun goes off and they commence running. Then what?"

"One of them arrives at the tape before the other," I said. "He is the winner, the other is the loser."

Again Aqua smiled. "We used to think like that."

"What changed your mind?"

"Take the rabbit you call the winner. How fast did he run in order to win the race?"

"I haven't any idea. What difference does it make? The point is that he ran faster than the loser, the other rabbit."

"Very well," Aqua said. "Take the loser. How fast did he run?"

"Again, I don't know. It doesn't matter. He is the loser because he runs more slowly than the winner."

"So we are back to the winner again. Let us imagine that he is A. Very well, if we ask how fast A runs, the only answer can be: A runs as fast as A runs. The same is true of B. B runs precisely as fast as B runs. Now you are suggesting that we compare these speeds. If A is declared the winner, if, as you put it, he runs faster than B, this can only be because we assume that A's speed, whatever it is, should be taken as the measure of B's."

"But why not assume that?"

Aqua hummed for a moment. "Wouldn't that be a bit arbitrary? After all, we could just as easily take B's speed as the measure of A's, and then A would lose because he had deviated from the norm, because his speed is greater than B's."

I rubbed my eyes. "No, A would win the race for that reason. Winning and losing speeds are relative, not absolute. The winner is faster than the loser, the loser is slower than the winner."

"But how would you characterize the speed of A? Comparatively speaking, it is, as you say, faster than B's. But might you not have asked: How fast did A run? You answer: faster than B. The question is asked once more: But how fast did A run? Your only answer can be: as fast as he ran.

It is because we have recognized this that we have set up the contests as we have. Surely you can see that it is perfectly logical."

Aqua turned away. I let him go. Something was askew in what he said, but I needed a moment to discover what it was. In search of solitude, I went aloft, soaring and gliding over and around the playing field. From a height, the various events below seemed doubly inconsequential. What was the point of this day with all its panoply and ballyhoo if all it managed to establish was that a creature was as fast as he was? Surely that is not something that awaits discovery or has to be established by a race.

How high did I fly? How long was I gone? Not idle questions, these; they take me to the heart of the matter. What Aqua's disquisition revealed was the lack of a common measure. As earlier in the case of the monetary system and the system of calculation, I saw that I was in a position to confer upon the animal kingdom a signal benefit. I could provide a measure of distance and velocity.

What, I asked myself, have humans devised as a system of measurement? If I said I had flown to a height of a thousand feet, the reference would seem to be to the pedal extremity of some human. My height was equivalent to a thousand times the unshod foot of a human being, heel to toe, heel to toe, high in the sky. But whose foot? An athlete's foot? That of the average human being? Surely not. A horse is said to be so many hands high, and the inch, as we know from French, is a thumb. Here, seemingly, was the kind of arbitrariness Aqua had been inveighing against. Can a foot be less than a foot in length? How long is an inchworm? Or take the metric system. What is a meter? How does this differ from asking, "What is a yard?" If you produce a yardstick, you are saying: here is a stick and it is a yard long, but where is the yard the stick is as long as? And where is the meter the meterstick is as long as? There is a straightforward answer to this last question.

In Paris, carefully kept under controlled conditions of temperature and moisture and the like, is a platinum-iridium bar which is *the* meter. It is the eponymous meter. Meter is its proper name. It is the object by comparison with which every other meter is a meter. So much for length.

The measure of velocity, the measure of the passage of time, the measure of motion, what is it? For most daily concerns, it is of course the sun. A day, an hour, a minute, a month, a season, a year—all these are computed with reference to the sun. Here was a possible solution to the dilemma of the games. I could construct a clock, an hourglass, a water clock, that would serve as the common standard of speed for the various contests. Here, writ small in a trickle of sand or water, would be the hegemony of the sun, the measure of our days and doings. This solemn cosmic thought was pushed aside. Pride, vanity, returned. My system of DO would be my guide. Just as a particular metal bar in Paris is paradigmatic of length throughout the world where the metric system is employed, what was needed was a measure of which it must be said: it is what it is. The velocity of the sun is the velocity of the sun. Other velocities are measured by its. What the animal kingdom needed was some similarly selected single thing by comparison with which the movements of other things could be measured. In the case of a metal bar, less so in the case of the sun, the selection was arbitrary. The animal kingdom, on the other hand, was fortunate to have me as a member. The answer to the problem was obvious. What animal is unique of its kind, at once singular and universal, wonderfully adapted to be the paradigm of speed? I banked and began a swift descent to the playing field.

Aqua listened to what I had to say, somewhat impatiently at first, but with growing interest. Others gathered round, drawn perhaps by the fervor with which I spoke. Green said excitedly, "It is a new application of DO."

"That's right."

"I'm for it."

Aqua conceded that this would allow those present to enter as many contests as they wished. He looked at me. "You of course will have to enter them all. To provide the standard."

"I know."

"Everything will have to be rerun, the field against Dormer the dodo."

There were some conservative protests but

these were overridden by the claque that had formed around Green and Purple.

The first race was staked out as I paced the field. It was to be the mDO dash, the DO being me from stem to stern. I returned to the starting line, fanned my wings several times and glanced up and down the line. The new arrangement had turned most of the participants into spectators.

Virgil the rabbit was on the line with me as well as an airedale I had not met. Aqua raised his pistol. A crack, and we were off. I flew as fast as I flew and the airedale and Virgil were well ahead of me. Not that it mattered. I could neither win nor lose. I was no more of an entrant than a stopwatch would

have been. And I was just as necessary. My speed, of course, was DO. The airedale had run it in DOg and the rabbit in DOgz. A snail, I later learned, managed the course in the respectable time of dDO. The award ceremony after this event was more festive than those I had seen earlier, but there was some grumbling. The crowd was used to praising winners, and losers were a novelty.

"Next the xDO race," Aqua announced, and I betook myself to the starting line.

There followed the hurdles, the relays, the

various jumps, the leaps, the throwing of the discus and hammer, the freestyle in the pool. Event after event, and I was a participant in them all. Weariness came over me, but I could not stop. A precedent was being established, history was being made. Some measure of immortality for my species was being assured by establishing the primacy of DO. I did not formulate the thought explicitly, but I am sure that what drove me was the prospect that, in future years, long after I, and with me my species, was gone, a tribute would be paid us in the form of the use of DO in these annual animal games. The meter was enshrined in Paris, the sun moves in the cold reaches of space, but for the forseeable future and beyond the dodo would be enshrined in the hearts of animals. There might even be dodo watches.

It was this that drove me through the day and brought me all but exhausted to the culminating event, the xxxxxDO race, formerly the marathon. I dragged myself to the starting line. Few others joined me there but among them was Virgil the rabbit and the still nameless airedale, both refreshed from sitting out several intervening contests.

"How do you feel, Dormer?" Aqua asked.

"I'm ready."

"This is the last event."

"I won't be going very swiftly, Aqua."

"You shall be quick as a dodo, Dormer, and that is all that matters."

"You're right, of course."

Aqua put us on our mark. Crouched, ready to go, perspiration running from my forehead, I wished that there was a wind to ride, something to make this race easier for me, but the only wind there was would be in my face for half the race. Despite the fortitude I feigned with Aqua, I wondered if I would be able to fly xxxxx times my length. But to withdraw was inconceivable. Can a stopwatch withdraw? Hardly. Without me there could be no race and this race was the crown of the day. Those not taking part, and this was the vast majority, were seated in the stands, ready to welcome the winner. I could not let down that expectant crowd.

Aqua lowered his left arm, indicating that he would fire soon. And then we were off. Weariness seemed to leave me as I left the ground and got

into the air. The repetitive activity of flying seemed something that could continue independently of will or strength. I'll make it, I told myself. I must make it. A dodo never quits.

Indeed, the farther I flew, the faster I flew. Below me I saw the airedale loping along with great bounding strides, effortlessly. He cast an eye up at me and his tongue lolled as if in a smile. An admirable beast. His name, I had learned, was Fritz. We left the playing field, with Virgil not far behind, and I rose to clear the copse of trees while Fritz and Virgil disappeared among the trees. The wind was fresh on my face now, and while this made flying difficult, it was refreshing, too.

The first time we passed the bleachers in the playing field, a great roar went up. A humming bird had dropped out so the field was down to

Fritz and Virgil and, of course, myself. Virgil was in the lead when we left the field, but Fritz overtook him and then once more I was over the copse of trees and they were in it. Fritz emerged first and, hitting his stride, moved out ahead of me. I looked back but there was no sign of Virgil. For a second time, Fritz and I went past the bleachers and for a second time a cheer went up, but it was a cheer with a question in it. What had happened to Virgil the rabbit? Had he overextended himself this day and fallen victim to his heart?

Over the copse once more and then, as I cleared it, I saw movement below. It was not Fritz. He was already free of the trees and streaking for the playing field and the end of the race. What I saw was Sidney, and he had a burlap bag slung over his shoulder. My first impulse was to swoop down on him, but I could not deprive Fritz of his winning time. I began to fly faster than I had flown all day. The roar of my wings drowned out the sound of the wind. Below me Fritz came into sight and I was gaining on him. When we entered the playing field, not quite together, he was still ahead, and those in the stands were on their feet. Their cheers lifted, spurring me on. I closed my eyes and headed for the finish line, giving everything I had. The rising roar told me when I was there. I opened my eyes and saw Fritz directly below. We had tied. Fritz had run the race in exactly DO.

He was surrounded immediately. He lay on the ground, panting. Aqua waved, beckoning me

Quick as a Dodo

down, but I had a further task. I lapped the field, taking a final cheer and then, with my heart beating frantically, headed once more out of the playing field and toward the copse of trees.

I landed among the trees to rest, to plan my strategy. It was clear to me what had happened. Sidney had laid a trap for Virgil, snared him, and taken him home. For some animals, this fate might not have been tragic, but I could not imagine that courageous little rabbit lying content in a slipper in Sidney's closet or, worse, penned up in a cage like Mr. Cheeps. He would long to be rescued, and that was obviously a job for me.

Meanwhile, I had to rest, to catch my breath, to get a drink. I decided to wait for dark. It would have been a great mistake to announce to the audience at the playing field what had happened to Virgil. In their wrath, they would have moved as one animal to the Morton house. The result would have been serious injury to some and capture for others, and it was doubtful that Virgil would have been freed in the process. No, this was a job for a single agent. This was a job for the dodo. It pained me to think what the others might

make of my absence. I had to run the risk of being thought a deserter at a crucial moment of the animal games.

The bed I made for myself was not unlike that in which I had hatched little Otto. Although I rejoiced that the little fellow had been united with his mother, I could not help feeling again the disappointment of knowing that I was indeed the only surviving dodo. Ah well.

I must concentrate now on rescuing Virgil. If I succeeded—and I meant to succeed—Virgil would be spared the oppressive solicitude of the human race, the cruel and insouciant companionship of Sidney, the exploitative schemes of George Morton. There may be some, though my reader will not be among them, who wonder if the fate of a single rabbit is worth the risk I would run in rescuing him. Such pusillanimity is as foreign to my nature as it is to yours. If the individual is unimportant, then no collection of individuals is important either. Zero added to zero is zero still. Virgil was important. His uniqueness differed from my own but it was uniqueness nonetheless. He was himself, Virgil, and no other rabbit could make that statement.

I napped but did not permit myself to fall into the deep sleep my weary body craved. There would come a time for sleep. Now, watchfulness was required. The sun set, darkness crept over the earth, the moon rose. The time had come. I got up, left the copse of trees, and moved stealthily in the direction of the Morton house.

At the picket fence bordering the yard, I stopped. There was a light on in Sidney's room, but otherwise the house was dark. Was Sidney reading in bed? It was possible. Did he have Virgil with him in his room? That seemed most likely. It would be like Sidney to keep his new pet a secret from his parents. I hopped to the top of the fence, then lifted into the air, flying directly to the fireplace chimney through which I had effected my own escape from the house. A way out is also a way in.

I must have lost weight from the exertions of the day because I slipped easily down the

chimney. When I emerged, I heard stirring from the cage of Mr. Cheeps. Of course the cage was covered for the night, but the sound of my final drop onto the grate of the fireplace wakened the little parakeet. I got on top of the cage and pulled off the cover.

"Don't be frightened, Mr. Cheeps. It is I."

"I can't see you."

"I am Dormer the dodo."

"Aha. So you've come back. Didn't like it out there, did you? Well, they took your cage away, so I don't know where you'll sleep. But at least it will be warm and dry."

"Would you please be still." The parakeet would have babbled himself to death if I hadn't stopped him. "Tell me, does Sidney have another pet?"

"I don't like Sidney. He pulls my tail."

"Did you see him bring home a pet today?"

"Another dodo?"

I bristled. "There is no other dodo."

"Why are you whispering?"

"My throat is sore."

"You're afraid the Mortons will hear you, aren't you?"

With that, the traitorous bird began to shout at the top of his lungs for Mrs. Morton. I tried to shut him up, but he was beyond argument now. I retrieved the cage cover from the floor where I had dropped it, but as I flew back to Mr. Cheeps' cage, I banged into a floor lamp and sent it, and myself, toppling. Mr. Cheeps subsided. I crept beneath a chair. We were both waiting and, sure enough, there were sounds upstairs.

"I heard something," Flo Morton said.

"You heard that blasted bird. So did I. He's quiet now."

"Something fell."

"Maybe he tipped his cage over."

"George! Please go down and see."

With much muttering and after some delay, George Morton came downstairs, turning on lights as he came; first the stair light, then the hall light, then the living room light, and finally the light in the sun porch.

"What's going on out here?" he demanded.

"The dodo's back. He tipped over the lamp. He's hiding under that chair."

"Stop your infernal chirping."

"Listen to me, you nitwit. The dodo is under that chair." Mr. Cheeps should have known better. Mr. Morton did not understand Parakeet. I had forgotten this myself and almost started to make a break for it when Cheeps began his treacherous talk. But I remembered in time and remained where I was.

"How did you tip over this lamp?" Morton grumbled, standing it up again.

"I didn't tip it over. The dodo did."

"Crazy bird," Morton said. "I don't know what Flo sees in you." And with that he dropped the cover on the cage, silencing Mr. Cheeps. I listened with relief to the sound of Morton leaving the room.

He detoured by the kitchen, and I heard the refrigerator door open. The sound reminded me that I was ravenously hungry. The thought of that refrigerator bursting with food made me tremble with desire. I was tempted to saunter into the kitchen, greet George Morton in a carefree way, and fly into the food. I would recite the Gettysburg Address willingly. I would say, "Polly want a cracker" on national television. Anything in exchange for food.

Courage, I was learning, is sometimes most decisively proved on a small field, in a skirmish rather than a battle. Hunger was my adversary. I had to combat my own appetite and the thought of all that food in the kitchen. Next to these, physical danger, the threat of capture, seemed mere bagatelles. I knew that if I could conquer my desire to raid the refrigerator, I would have crossed a Rubicon in the building of my moral character.

So I lay sweating on the floor under a chair, steeling myself to creep, when the coast was clear, past the kitchen and upstairs to Sidney's room. I had no doubt now that Virgil was there. I must not go into the kitchen. To give in to my hunger would be to desert caution altogether. I would not bother to be quiet if I unleashed the beast in myself. It was certain as sin that Morton would hear me, creep down, and capture me, and that meant the end for both myself and Virgil the rabbit.

Eventually, Morton returned upstairs, and all the lights were out. The house fell silent. I crept from under the chair and walked swiftly through

the house to the stairs. The kitchen was to my left now, but I had wiped it from my mind. And then the motor of the refrigerator switched on, and the familiar hum that had drawn me from my slipper to a midnight snack filled my ears. Sweat stood out on my forehead. Against my will, my body began

to turn toward the kitchen, as if I were magne-
tized and the refrigerator with its food was north.
I gripped the railing, shaking my head violently.
True north lay upstairs. I began to ascend. With
each step, it became easier. I made it.

I was in the upstairs hallway. There was a
thin ribbon of light under Sidney's door. I went
rapidly to the door and stood there, my ear to the
panel, listening. I heard the rustle of bed clothes, I
seemed to hear Sidney's even breathing. And then
I heard something else. A nibbling noise. Slowly I
opened the door and let myself into Sidney's room.

The loathsome boy was indeed asleep, lying
on his back, one arm outthrown, his mouth open. I
turned to the closet. Its door was open. In it was
the cage George Morton had put me in. Its current

occupant was Virgil the rabbit. He was nibbling on a large head of lettuce. The nibbling stopped when he saw me. I put a finger to my bill. His nose wriggled in understanding.

The lock of the cage presented no difficulty to one on the outside. I opened the door and Virgil squeezed free. Sidney slept on. I nodded toward the hallway and opened the door. Virgil hopped into the hallway, and immediately a piercing scream rent the air. It was Mrs. Morton. She must have just come out of her room. Sidney rose from his bed as if it had been detonated. George Morton tumbled onto the floor, at least from the sound of it. And Mrs. Morton's scream rose higher.

"Dormer!" Sidney said behind me.

"Farewell," I cried and into the hall I charged. Virgil was nowhere in sight. Flo Morton, her nightgown held high, spinning, still screaming, turned and caught sight of me. How her scream became more shrill it is given to neither dodo nor man to know. Perhaps to dogs. Then she slumped to the floor. Emerging from his room, Morton tripped over the fallen body of his wife. His eyes fell on me as he fell on the floor, and his expression changed from panic to delight. I flew past him, headed for the stairs. Virgil was in the kitchen, crouched by the back door, his little body atremble with fear. I could almost hear the pulsations of his heart. I fumbled with the lock, finally turned it, and pulled opened the door. "Scoot," I cried to Virgil. "Scoot."

And scoot he did. Just as his tail cleared the

doorway a hand closed on my shoulder and pulled me back into the kitchen. The door slammed. I

turned and looked up into the triumphant smile of George Morton.

❋

No words can describe the emotions with which one hears the door of his jail close behind him. It has been months now since I heard that sound. I am well-fed and watered; nothing short of freedom is denied me. Mr. Cheeps insists that this is bliss. I know better. Nor do I confuse my fame, or notoriety, with the meaning of life. Buckley praised my repartee when I appeared on "Firing Line," as well he might. He opined that I was not the first dodo who had sat in the chair I occupied. But surely I was the first guest who had been tied in his chair. I have been interviewed and feted. A committee of ornithologists, with only one dissenting vote—that of Professor Sisson—certified my claim to be a dodo. I speak to conservation groups, to birdwatcher clubs, to scout troops, and to congressional committees. Everywhere I plead for my freedom. Everywhere I am ignored. I have been declared a planetary asset by the U.N., that connoisseur of assets, too valuable to be permitted to govern my own life. I must be guarded, I must be kept safe, I must continue to live in captivity. George Morton, such are the *lacrimae rerum*, has enlisted the world on his side.

At least the world of men. Whatever Mr. Cheeps, that poor domesticated bird, may say, no animal would confuse the life I lead with happiness. It is humiliating to be introduced as the only dodo in captivity. I shall never acquiesce to my fate. I watch my chance. I will not rest until I am once more free. My ancestors, on those islands east of Madagascar, died out before the advance of European settlers. By some miracle, I escaped the common fate. I shall continue to escape it. I live in the conviction that, one day, Dormer the dodo will again clear the picket fence in the Morton back-yard and rise into the freedom of flight. Unrealistic? Sidney is out as an accomplice, I know. But

Flo Morton is another story. I depend on her animosity. I may yet feel the boost of her broom and the sound of her "Shoo" as I begin my flight to freedom.